Bks due
7/5/2013

Bright and Early Books

Bright and Early Books are an offspring of the world-famous Beginner Books...designed for *an even lower age group*. Making ingenious use of humor, rhythm, and limited vocabulary, they will encourage even pre-schoolers to discover the delights of reading for themselves.

For other Bright and Early titles, see the back endpapers.

BRIGHT and EARLY BOOKS for BEGINNING Beginners

Copyright © 1996 by Jon Buller and Susan Schade.
All rights reserved under International and Pan-American Copyright
Conventions. Published in the United States by Random House, Inc., New York,
and simultaneously in Canada by Random House of Canada Limited, Toronto.

http://www.randomhouse.com/

Library of Congress Cataloging-in-Publication Data
Schade, Susan.
Snow bugs / by Susan Schade and Jon Buller.
   p.   cm. — (Bright & early book ; BE 29)
SUMMARY: The snow bugs discover wonderful ways to play on a snowy day.
ISBN 0-679-87913-7 (trade) — ISBN 0-679-97913-1 (lib. bdg.)
[1. Snow—Fiction. 2. Insects—Fiction. 3. Stories in rhyme.]
I. Buller, Jon, 1943–   . II. Title. III. Series.
PZ8.3. S287S1   1997
[E]—dc20
96-14239

Printed in the United States of America   10 9 8 7 6 5 4 3 2 1

SNOW BUGS

by Susan Schade and Jon Buller

A Bright & Early Book

From BEGINNER BOOKS

A Division of Random House, Inc.

It's snowing.
It's blowing.

It's a snow day!

It's a play day!

Roll over and slide.

Throw snowballs and hide.

It's freezing!

They're sneezing.

Run back inside!

Bugs who are bare
need something to wear.

Find some wool.
Cut and pull.

Sit and knit.

Does it fit?

A sweater for Fran.
A sweater for Ann.

A blue scarf for Ed.
A green hat for Fred.

A snowsuit for Dot.
Four mittens for Spot.

Are we ready?
No, not yet.
This is what
we need to get...

a leather strip,
a paper clip,

a toothpick,
an ice cream stick,

a broken spoon,
a piece of string.

"Hop in, Dot,
that's everything!"

Oh, no!
TOO much snow!

What to do?
Shovel through!

Pulling and pushing.

Slipping . . .

and whooshing.

Sliding, gliding, riding.

WHEEEE!

High and low.

Fast and slow.

Scoop and throw.

Ho, ho, ho!

Flap your wings.

Make snow things.

Then at night,
by candlelight...

a BUGS-ON-ICE SHOW!

Go, Dot, go!

Watch her score
a perfect ten.

"Hooray, Dot, skate again!"

Show bugs! Snow bugs!

Way to go, bugs!

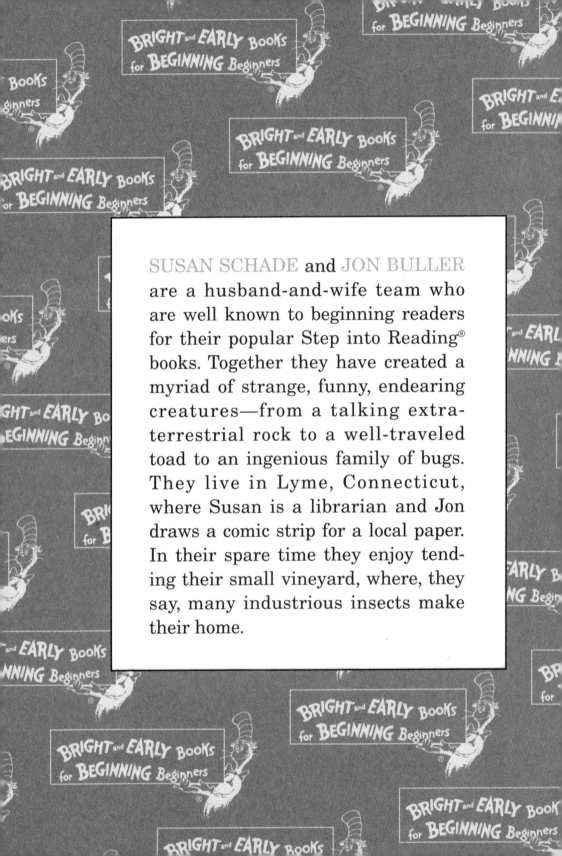

SUSAN SCHADE and JON BULLER
are a husband-and-wife team who
are well known to beginning readers
for their popular Step into Reading®
books. Together they have created a
myriad of strange, funny, endearing
creatures—from a talking extra-
terrestrial rock to a well-traveled
toad to an ingenious family of bugs.
They live in Lyme, Connecticut,
where Susan is a librarian and Jon
draws a comic strip for a local paper.
In their spare time they enjoy tend-
ing their small vineyard, where, they
say, many industrious insects make
their home.

Other Bright and Early Books You Will Enjoy

by Susan Schade and Jon Buller
SNUG HOUSE, BUG HOUSE

by Marc Brown
WINGS ON THINGS

by Dr. Seuss
GREAT DAY FOR UP
MARVIN K. MOONEY WILL YOU PLEASE GO NOW!
MR. BROWN CAN MOO! CAN YOU?
THE SHAPE OF ME AND OTHER STUFF
THERE'S A WOCKET IN MY POCKET!

by Stan & Jan Berenstain
THE BERENSTAIN BEARS ON THE MOON
HE BEAR, SHE BEAR
INSIDE, OUTSIDE, UPSIDE DOWN
THE BERENSTAIN BEARS
 AND THE SPOOKY OLD TREE
OLD HAT, NEW HAT